LITTLE GREY RABBIT'S
BIRTHDAY

LITTLE GREY RABBIT'S BIRTHDAY

By Alison Uttley
Pictures by Margaret Tempest

templar publishing

SQUIRREL AND HARE were gardening one fine day. "It's Little Grey Rabbit's birthday on Midsummer Day," said Squirrel. "We must give her a nice present."

"A very nice present," agreed Hare. "A cake or something. Something we can all share."

"Yes, a birthday cake with candles on it," said Squirrel.

"I don't like the taste of candles," objected Hare.

"They're not to eat!" cried Squirrel. "They are to show how old you are. Three candles if you are three years old."

"And a hundred if you are a hundred years old," said Hare. "Oh, Squirrel, can we make the cake ourselves?"

"I think so," nodded Squirrel. "But it must be a secret."

Just then Grey Rabbit came running out of the house.

"Grey Rabbit," said Hare. "Squirrel and I have been saying that it will be your b-b—"

"Shh! Not a word!" whispered Squirrel.

"No! It's a secret," said Hare hastily.

"A secret from me?" asked Grey Rabbit.

"It's something that mustn't be told," said Hare with importance.

"You are a funny pair," laughed Grey Rabbit.

"Will you come for a walk to visit the Speckledy Hen? I want some eggs for tea."

"We'll come, won't we Hare?" said Squirrel, throwing down the rake.

They went through the field where Moldy Warp lived.

"Hello!" he cried when the three friends arrived.

"This is a surprise." He hurried to fetch glasses of heather ale and brought them outside.

"I'm going to tell," Hare suddenly exclaimed. "I can't keep the secret in. I shall burst!"

"No! No!" cried Squirrel, shaking his arm.

"Come inside, and whisper it to me and the doorpost," said Mole kindly. Hare followed him into the passage.

"It's Grey Rabbit's birthday on Midsummer Day, and we are going to make a cake," he said breathlessly.

"Ah! That is a good secret!" agreed Mole. "I'll give her a present."

"And come to tea with us," said Hare.

"Thank you, Hare," said Mole.

The three friends said goodbye and Grey
Rabbit led the way through the wood to the
great tree where Owl lived.

Squirrel ran up the tree and called softly through the open window.

"Wise Owl! It's Grey Rabbit's birthday on Midsummer Day."

"Gr-gr-gr," snored Wise Owl, but he heard in his dreams all the same.

They passed into the fields where Hedgehog was coming back from milking.

"Can we have a drink?" asked Squirrel, dancing up to him. "It's thirsty work keeping secrets."

Hare took Old Hedgehog aside and whispered, "It's Grey Rabbit's birthday on Midsummer Day. We are going to make her a cake, and you can come and taste it."

"Ah! Thank ye!" cried Hedgehog.

"Come along, Hare. We shall never get to the Speckledy Hen's house," called Grey Rabbit, "if you spend all the time telling secrets."

When they arrived at the farm, there was the Speckledy Hen walking about.

"We've come for some eggs, Speckledy Hen," said Grey Rabbit.

While the Hen was filling up the basket, Hare whispered in her ear.

"It's Grey Rabbit's birthday on Midsummer Day. We are going to make a cake, and you can come and taste it."

"I'll bring a present for dear Grey Rabbit," whispered Hen.

The next day Squirrel and Hare decided to make the cake.

"We must do it secretly," said Hare. "Won't Grey Rabbit be surprised! She doesn't know we can make cakes."

"We don't know either," muttered Squirrel.

"Grey Rabbit! Go away!" commanded Hare, when Little Grey Rabbit came in from the garden.

"Oh Hare! What have I done? What's the matter?" Her ears drooped and a tear came into her eye.

Squirrel stamped her foot. "Hare! How stupid you are!' she exclaimed. She wiped Grey Rabbit's eyes, and said kindly, "Grey Rabbit! Please will you take a bottle of primrose wine to Wise Owl? He was hooting

last night. Moldy Warp would like a visit,
and I am sure Fuzzypeg would love to hear
a story."

"Then I'll run off at once," said Grey Rabbit, smiling at her two friends.

"Goodbye!" called Squirrel and Hare, and they waved their paws as Grey Rabbit went along the lane.

"Quickly! Quickly!" cried Hare.

Squirrel sniffed
at all the jars of
spices and herbs
on the dresser.

"Here's tansy and woodruff, and preserved
violets and bottled cherries,' she said.

"Here's poppyseed and acorns and beech
nuts," said Hare. "Oh, here's the pepper pot.
How much shall I put in?"

"A fistful of everything makes a nice cake,"
said Squirrel.

So they dipped their paws into every
jar, and mixed the seeds and herbs in the
yellow bowl.

"Is the oven hot?" said a deep voice.
There at the window was Old Hedgehog
watching them with twinkling eyes.

"I comed with extra milk for the cake,"
said he. "You didn't ought to put pepper in
it."

Hare blushed and tried to hide the pepper
pot.

"Oh Hare! We shall have to begin all over
again," said Squirrel.

"I'll come and lend a hand," said Old
Hedgehog.

He made up the fire and showed Squirrel
how to mix the sugar and butter together
and how to sprinkle in the currants and spices.

Hare ran to the garden and brought in
rose petals and violets – all the sweet-smelling
things he could find to add to the cake.
He beat up the eggs till they were a yellow
froth, and Hedgehog dropped them into
the mixture.

"Now I must be off," said Hedgehog. "Remember not to open the oven door till the good rich smell comes out."

They popped the cake in the hot oven and shut the door.

After a while there came a strong sweet smell.

"The cake!" Hare cried. "It's telling us it's ready to come out."

So Squirrel wrapped a cloth round her paw and lifted out the good-smelling cake, as brown as a berry, all puffed up and crinkly with sugar and spices.

They carried it into the garden and hid it under an empty beehive.

The next day when Grey Rabbit had gone out to gather wool from the hedges, Squirrel ran to the garden for the cake. She iced it and wrote:

Grey Rabbit's Birthday

on the top in the pollen dust.

Hare put lots of candles round the edge – big candles, little candles, red and blue and green ones – and then they danced for joy. "It is fit for a fairy queen," they told each other.

They hid the cake in the beehive again, ready for Midsummer Day.

"I'm going to make a fan for Grey Rabbit," said Squirrel. "I shall ask the green woodpecker and the goldfinch for some feathers."

"And I will make a purse for her," said Hare.

Squirrel begged a few feathers from the birds. She put them together, and there was the prettiest little fan of green and gold.

Hare went to the pasture for a puff-ball. He washed the little bag in the dew, then he tied it with ribbon-grasses.

Darkness came and the three little animals went upstairs to bed.

In the night Grey Rabbit was wakened by a faint noise under her window. She slipped out of bed, and putting her cloak over her nightgown, ran downstairs and into the garden.

There, crouched in a sad, prickly little ball, was Fuzzypeg.

"What's the matter, Fuzzypeg?" whispered Grey Rabbit.

"I comed to say Happy Birthday," said Fuzzypeg.

"I got out of the window, and I runned very fast, but I heard Wise Owl hooting, and I got frightened."

"Poor little Fuzzypeg," said Grey Rabbit softly. "You had better come into my bed."

She took his paw and led him upstairs.

"I knew you'd take care of me, Grey Rabbit. Happy Birthday."

"It isn't my birthday till tomorrow, Fuzzypeg," said Grey Rabbit.

She tucked him up, then she wrapped her cloak round herself and crept under the bed. She couldn't sleep with a bundle of prickles by her side.

The next morning Hare and Squirrel raced downstairs to get the breakfast.

"I'm going to say Happy Birthday to Grey Rabbit," said Hare.

"So am I," said Squirrel.

"I shall say it first because I'm bigger than you," said Hare.

"No, I shall say it first because I'm the little one," said Squirrel.

They stared at each other crossly.

"Let's both say it together," said Squirrel.

So upstairs they bundled, and they flung open the bedroom door.

"Happy Birthday!" came squeaking from the bed, and out of the blankets came Fuzzypeg's dark head.

"I said it first!" said he.

The noise wakened Grey Rabbit, and she crawled out from under the bed.

Hare and Squirrel were so surprised, they never said Happy Birthday at all. They just stared and stared.

"Milk-o!" the call came from the kitchen.
"Has anyone seen our Fuzzypeg? He runned
away in the night, and it's my belief he came
to see Miss Grey Rabbit."

"Here he is, Hedgehog!" they shouted,
running downstairs.

"I said it first," boasted Fuzzypeg. "I said
Happy Birthday before any of you."

"He said he would be the first and he's done it," said Old Hedgehog proudly.

"Let him stay for breakfast," pleaded Grey Rabbit, and Hedgehog agreed.

Soon they all sat round the table and ate the nice food.

"It's your birthday, Grey Rabbit," said Squirrel. "So you shall have a holiday. We'll wash up the cups and plates."

"Then I'll go into the garden with Fuzzypeg and show him the flowers," said Grey Rabbit.

When they came to the beehive a stream of honeybees flew out.

"Hare! Squirrel! A swarm of bees is living in our empty hive," called Grey Rabbit. "Isn't it exciting? Listen, they are humming something."

This is what they heard:

> *"It's Grey Rabbit's Birthday,*
> *She doesn't want money*
> *Or fine clothes or riches.*
> *We'll make her some honey."*

Hare and Squirrel looked at one another and sighed. "Honey out of our cake," they whispered.

At four o'clock Squirrel and Hare sent Grey Rabbit upstairs, while they got ready the tea. Then they ran down the garden to the beehive.

They lifted up the straw skep, and there was the cake, looking nicer than ever. Around it were little pots of honey, each as big as a thimble.

They carried the treasures indoors and placed them on the table. Grey Rabbit came running downstairs.

What a surprise! The table was beautiful with the birthday cake and all the candles alight upon it. The tiny pots of honey shone like gold, and there were dishes of cresses and nuts and cream.

"Oh! Oh!" cried Grey Rabbit. "What's this?"

"It's somebody's birthday cake," said Squirrel.

"It's everybody's cake, and here they come to the feast," said Hare.

Up the path came many little feet. Then there was a rat-tat-tat at the door.

"Come in! Come in!" cried Squirrel.

In trooped Moldy Warp, the Hedgehog family, the Speckledy Hen and a crowd of little animals.

"Many Happy Returns, Grey Rabbit," they cried. They saw the table, the lighted cake and the honey pots.

Then Squirrel gave Grey Rabbit the little fan made of feathers and Hare brought out the purse tied with green ribbon-grass.

Everybody had brought a present, but Moldy Warp's present was the best of all. It was the song of the nightingale in a tiny musical box.

They were all listening to the music, when the door was pushed open and a pair of large blinking eyes appeared.

"I won't come in," hooted Wise Owl, "but I have brought a small token of my regard for Grey Rabbit."

He thrust one claw forward and dropped a book on the table. Then he drifted away as silently as he had come.

"Whew!" exclaimed Moldy Warp. "That was a shock."

"What has he brought?" asked Hare.

"It's called *Wise Owl's Guide to Knowledge*," said Grey Rabbit, holding the tiny green volume.

"Cut the cake, Grey Rabbit!" called Hare. "I'm hungry. Cut the cake!"

So Grey Rabbit cut the beautiful birthday cake and they all had a piece. It was as nice as it looked. Really, Hare and Squirrel had made it very well!

Moldy Warp drank Grey Rabbit's health, Squirrel recited a little poem, and Hare played a tune on his flute.

They all laughed and sang and danced till night came, and then they went home by the light of the moon.

"What a lovely birthday it has been," said Grey Rabbit. "How kind everybody is to me!"

She looked at all the little treasures the woodland folk had brought.

Then she went upstairs to bed, with the musical box under her arm. She turned the handle and the voice of the nightingale came trilling out. From the woods another nightingale answered.

"A Happy Birthday, Grey Rabbit," it seemed to say. "Thank you for all the fun you give us."

WHICH LITTLE GREY RABBIT BOOKS DO YOU HAVE?

THE SQUIRREL, THE HARE AND THE LITTLE GREY RABBIT

By Alison Uttley
Pictures by Margaret Tempest

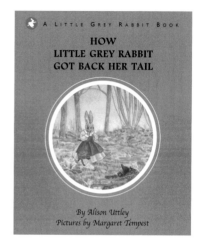

HOW LITTLE GREY RABBIT GOT BACK HER TAIL

By Alison Uttley
Pictures by Margaret Tempest

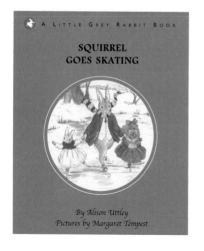

SQUIRREL GOES SKATING

By Alison Uttley
Pictures by Margaret Tempest

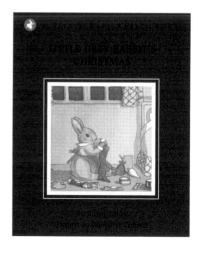

LITTLE GREY RABBIT'S CHRISTMAS

By Alison Uttley
Pictures by Margaret Tempest

A LITTLE GREY RABBIT BOOK

LITTLE GREY RABBIT'S VALENTINE

By Alison Uttley
Pictures by Margaret Tempest

A LITTLE GREY RABBIT BOOK

HARE AND THE EASTER EGGS

By Alison Uttley
Pictures by Margaret Tempest

A LITTLE GREY RABBIT BOOK

LITTLE GREY RABBIT'S BIRTHDAY

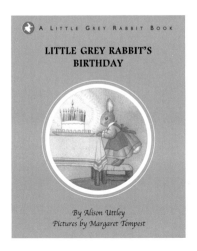

By Alison Uttley
Pictures by Margaret Tempest

A LITTLE GREY RABBIT BOOK

THE STORY OF FUZZYPEG THE HEDGEHOG

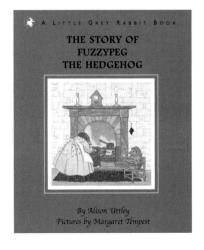

By Alison Uttley
Pictures by Margaret Tempest

A TEMPLAR BOOK

This edition first published in the UK in 2015 by Templar Publishing,
an imprint of The Templar Company Limited,
Deepdene Lodge, Deepdene Avenue, Dorking, Surrey, RH5 4AT, UK
www.templarco.co.uk

Original edition first published in the UK in 1944
by William Collins Sons & Co Ltd

This edition edited by *Susan Dickinson* and *Katie Haworth*
Additional design by *janie louise hunt*

1 3 5 7 9 10 8 6 4 2

ISBN 978-1-78370-232-9

Printed in China